MYSTERY AT POINT BEACH

~ Book 1 ~

Sundae Wars

Kate Jungwirth

Deborah Erdmann

Printed in the United States of America

First Printing, 2017

ISBN-9781728822754

This book is a work of fiction. All characters are fictitious, though the location is real. Some of the details inspired by local history and lore may have been added or altered to fit the story.

Cover design by: Henry Kiryowa Luja and Kawooya Tonny of Bulamu Art Community

This book is dedicated to:

Dominic, the inspiration
for this story ~DE

My mother, who always read to me
when I was young ~ KJ

CHAPTER 1

"Dominator to GB ... Come in GB. Over."

"... Come in, GB."

"Dominic, Grandpa's honking the horn outside," Mom yelled up the stairs. "Can you hurry up before he wakes the entire neighborhood?"

"Be right there!" I shouted, stuffing my walkie-talkie into my backpack. Sliding down the banister from the second floor to the first, I was greeted by a scowl.

"Dominic Dorsey! How many times have I told you to walk down the stairs like regular people? That railing's wobbly the way it is."

"Geez, sorry Mom." I reached for my baseball cap and rushed to the door.

"Aren't you forgetting something?" She folded her arms. I gave her a quick hug.

"Come on, Dominic. Let's get this show on the road!" Grandpa Bob hollered as I hurried outside.

This was our annual camping trip to Point Beach, and he sure seemed eager to get back. I suspect the reason he insisted on traveling at the break of dawn was so no one would notice his Stone Age pop-up camper. Bold orange and brown lettering proclaimed the word "Nimrod" on each side.

I hefted my bike into the truck bed. After a couple of pats on my back from GB, we waved goodbye to Mom and headed off. Grandpa Bob likes the nickname GB because it also stands for "Green Bay," where we live, but more importantly, it's home to the Green Bay Packers—our favorite football team.

We cruised down the road listening to polka classics almost as old as the camper, which made the short forty-five-minute drive seem like an eternity. When we finally arrived at the campground, GB turned off the music, but the accordion still played in my head.

At the park entrance, a stick of a man in a hat too big for his head waited at the window to check us in.

With arms crossed, the ranger narrowed his gaze at our camper. Looking back at us, he snickered, "I think I've seen this Nimrod before—on the cover of *Junkyard Salvage* magazine."

Nimrod is another word for fool, so it didn't throw me for a curve when the ranger eyed us as we pulled up to the window. Grandpa Bob, on the other hand, refused to take any guff.

"You must be new here." GB leaned over to read the ranger's identification. "Officer Rick, do us a favor and save your jokes for the campers with less imagination." He smoothed a few surviving strands of silver hair across his head.

"Don't you worry." The ranger reached out from the window with our tag. "I keep a tight watch over this campground, and I'll be keeping both my eyes on you, Mister." His stare shifted toward me. "You *and* your Nimrod."

As we pulled out, GB mumbled under his breath, "Yeah, well I'm keeping my eyes on you too, Ranger Rick."

GB liked to speak his mind, but I shrank back in my seat. I decided right then and there to win the lottery so I could buy Grandpa Bob an RV from this century.

Nimrod creaked and groaned all the way to site #127, our favorite campsite. It provided privacy with the added amenities of water, electricity, and the Lake Michigan beach right behind it. I had built a fort there last summer out of evergreen branches and driftwood, and couldn't wait to see if it survived, but first we needed to maneuver Nimrod onto our site.

GB handed me a walkie-talkie, bellowing orders into his as he slowly backed the truck. I tried to direct him from my end. "Left … no, Grandpa, left."

After nearly sideswiping a tree the size of Africa, GB decided to go left and finally snuggled Nimrod safely beneath the pines. He hopped out of the truck strutting and swaggering like a peacock. "You see how you do that, Dominic?"

I nodded. "Yup. Fits like a glove."

We celebrated our success with an Orange Crush soda pop, my favorite.

"Can I check things out now?" I pulled my bike down from the truck bed.

"We just got here. Give me a hand before you take off."

I don't think GB understood 11 year-old energy. I slammed my Crush and helped him crank up the camper. After we unloaded all the supplies, I hopped on my metallic, lime-green, ten-speed Trek and sped off.

As I cruised down Red Pine Trail I started whistling a polka tune I'd heard on the way up, called, "Who Stole the Kishka." It's not that I liked polkas, but who could resist a tune that joked about sausages and butcher shops? Once you hear a song like that, there's no getting it out of your head.

I had just rounded a curve when someone yelled, "Watch it, Nimrod!"

Too late. I collided into Ranger Rick, knocking him to the ground and sending a pair of binoculars flying out of his hands. Gripping the handle bar, I carefully untangled my front wheel from his legs.

"Where did *you* come from?" I stood there, shaking in my sneakers at the sight of him.

"I'll ask the questions around here, kid." He frowned, slowly getting back on his feet. "The question is—where did *you* come from?"

Still stunned, I backed up slowly, offering an apology. "Sorry, Ranger. I didn't see you."

"You can stuff your sorry in a sack. You ruined my uniform," he sniveled, brushing off the dirt. "I just had it dry-cleaned yesterday."

A park ranger who has an aversion to dirt—that's rich.

"Get lost, kid." He focused his beady eyes on me, then reached for his binoculars.

Fine with me. I bolted back toward camp. Somehow, I doubted Ranger Rick was birdwatching. More likely he was spying on some unsuspecting campers.

I got back to our site feeling hungry after that confrontation. GB was still inside Nimrod setting things up, so I started rummaging through a bag of snacks on the picnic table.

"Dominic, is that you trying to sneak some cookies?" GB hollered from inside the camper. I backed away when he stepped outside.

"I'm going to cook some brats and weenies on the grill, and I don't want you spoiling your appetite." He removed the bag from my reach.

"I wouldn't worry about that," I said. "If I spoil this one, there's sure to be another one right behind it."

GB relented and tossed me the package of cookies. "Okay, but only a few."

"Thanks, Grandpa. I'm going to check out the beach now."

"Just stay out of trouble," GB warned.

"Sure, as long as Ranger Rick quits appearing out of nowhere. I had a head-on collision with him on my bike. Now he really has it in for me."

"Some people in uniform get all puffed up."

"No, I'm serious," I explained, my mouth full of cookies. "I was whistling 'Who Stole the Kishka,' and he seemed to take it personally."

GB laughed. "Well, maybe he's hot on the trail of

the guy who stole the kishka, and doesn't want you in-terfering." He retired to a folding chair.

After my fill of cookies, I climbed over the hill behind our site to check out my secret fort. I breathed a sigh of relief at the sight of it still standing amid the sand dunes.

All was well with the world. That is—until I heard voices coming from inside.

CHAPTER 2

Someone was in my fort.

A sick sensation hit my stomach, which could be from eating too many cookies, but still. I strategically crept up on the intruders, worried they might hear me coming, until I realized I was sneaking around on a sand dune. How loud could it be?

"*Hi-yaaaah!*" I sprang through the willows, landing in a heap in front of the fort. I quickly jumped to my feet to see if I had scared them off.

A boy and a girl about my age stared back at me, wide-eyed. I can't say that I blamed them.

"What do you think you're doing in my fort?" I demanded, hands on hips.

"I'm sorry. We didn't see your name on it," the boy spouted back.

"Don't mind my brother. He's a hothead."

After they stepped outside, I noted their sandy hair and eyes as blue as Lake Michigan. The girl's hair hung almost to her knees, and even her brother's hair was long for a boy.

"No problem. I hope I didn't scare you. It's just that I built this fort last year, and I like to use it as a hangout. I didn't think anyone else knew about it." They looked harmless enough, even though the boy had a bit of an attitude. I extended my hand to them and introduced myself. "I'm Dominic."

The boy grabbed my hand first. "I'm Forest, and this is my sister, Sailor."

"Those are names you don't hear every day," I remarked.

"I was born in the woods, and Sailor was born on a boat. Our mother believes nature picked our names for us."

"Huh. Doesn't your mom believe in hospitals?" I chuckled. "Well, that might be a good thing. Otherwise your names might be Doctor and Nurse."

We all shared a good laugh. "So where are you

guys from?" I asked, wondering if maybe they wanted to be friends.

"We're from Chicago." Sailor tucked her hair behind her ears, knelt down into the soft sand, and started drawing pictures with a stick.

"Apparently, that's the wrong side of the tracks," Forest scoffed, "at least as far as the park ranger's concerned. He's been watching us with binoculars all day."

"Ranger Rick?" So *that's* who he was watching. "I think he has it in for me and my grandpa, too. He's shifty—reminds me of a raccoon with those dark circles under his eyes."

"Oh, yeah … like a thief." Forest added.

"So, are you guys camping here?"

Sailor nodded. "Yep. We're here with our grandma on the group site. Which site are you on?"

"What a coincidence. I'm camping with my grandpa." I pointed up the hill. "Come on. I'll show you, but you can't make fun of the Nimrod."

"Your grandpa's a nimrod?" Forest asked.

"No, that's the kind of camper we have. It's …

been around for a while." My face reddened.

Blasted Nimrod.

I quickly changed the subject. "We have lots of Orange Crush if you're thirsty."

"I'm in." Forest darted halfway up the hill with Sailor on his heels. It didn't take much to persuade those two.

As we got closer, I saw GB poking and prodding away at a charcoal grill. Wispy curls of smoke escaped here and there. Cooking meat was a science to be mastered, as far as he was concerned. He took off his weathered sun hat and wiped the sweat beads from his brow.

"Well, who do we have here?"

"Grandpa Bob, these are my friends, Forest and Sailor." I handed them each an Orange Crush from the cooler. "They're camping with their grandma."

"Those are names you don't hear every day." GB tipped back his head.

Forest and Sailor just smiled and nodded.

GB proceeded to load the table with food, probably wondering if he had enough to share with our guests. "Who's hungry?" he finally offered.

"I am," said Sailor. "Windsong isn't much for cooking, especially meat."

GB scratched his head. "Wind … what?"

"Our grandma." Sailor took a sip of her Orange Crush. "She likes everything to be organic."

GB shook his head, then folded his hands and closed his eyes. "We want to thank you, Lord, for this beautiful day and for the food You have blessed us with."

Sailor followed up with a hearty, "Amen!"

GB's eyebrows rose a few times as he watched Forest and Sailor eat like there was no tomorrow. Grabbing a newspaper, he relocated to a chair near the fire pit, leaving the clean-up to me.

"Dominic, when you're all done I think we'll bike into town. I want to see what they have at the Two Rivers Farmers Market."

"But isn't that, like, five miles away?" Sailor gasped.

GB grinned at her. "Missy, even old geezers like me can ride a bike."

"Really?" Forest's eyes widened.

"I rode my bike across the state last summer. My legs are as strong as rocks." He pounded on his calf muscles to prove it.

Forest shrugged. "I guess that's possible. Windsong can still do all kinds of yoga tricks."

Before GB had a chance to embarrass me any further, I pointed to the caption on the front page of the newspaper. "What's *that* all about?"

ICE CREAM BANDITS GET AWAY
WITH A SCOOP OF LOOT

GB skimmed through the article. "Looks like two men in ski masks broke into the Historic Washington House museum and ice cream parlor last night. They took off with money and some important historical items." He looked up. "I wonder who on earth would want to do that?"

"Yeah—why didn't they just take the ice cream? Duh." Sailor licked her lips at the mention of it.

Now everyone's eyebrows rose.

For the hundredth time, I looked down the Rawley Point bike trail to see if GB was anywhere in sight. A nagging feeling told me he had crossed paths with Ranger Rick. I could picture GB getting a citation for pedaling 12-mph in a 10-mph zone. At the very least, I should've warned him not to whistle any polka tunes.

I hopped off my bike and reached for my water bottle. Just as I began to take a swig, GB rolled into view.

"Sorry, Dominic. I saw a black-capped chickadee and stopped to take a few pictures."

"Well, it sure took you long enough. Race ya to the end of the trail!" I jumped on my bike and sped off.

"You're on! Loser washes dishes."

Even with a good head start, GB quickly caught up and then cruised past me almost effortlessly. A burst of adrenaline coursed through my body. I wasn't about to let this old coot stick me with the dishes.

Leaning forward, I pedaled furiously, leaving GB in a cloud of dust. Wiping the sweat from my eyes, I saw the trailhead sign up ahead. After crossing it, I stopped along the sidewalk, dead tired.

GB was only inches behind. "Well, Dom, looks like I'm doing dishes tonight."

I hate to admit it, but I think he let me win.

By the time we got to the Farmers Market in Central Park, the sun blazed hotter than ever. Still exhausted, I took a seat on a metal bench while GB scoured the produce stands.

Nearby, a large, brown historical marker with the words "ICE CREAM SUNDAE" written across the top caught my attention.

What's this? I got up to take a closer look.

White carved letters read that in 1881, a man named Ed Berners created the first ice cream sundae at his soda fountain shop right here in Two Rivers. No wonder the robbery was big news. This town sure took pride in their sundaes.

Suddenly, two police cars rounded the corner of 17th and Washington Street right in front of me.

CHAPTER 3

I watched down the block to see what the police were up to. The squad cars pulled over next to a tan, three-story building with blue trim. The sign on the building read: Historic Washington House.

I wanted to see what was going on, but knowing GB, he'd say that was interfering. I would need to find a better way to get him to take a slight detour.

Spotting GB at the strawberry stand was easy, thanks to his fluorescent orange-and-green-checkered shirt and army-green khakis. I could get past that part of the outfit, but sandals *and* socks? That's just wrong.

I walked my bike toward him. "Can we get some ice cream? I need energy for the ride back."

"What you need is some air in those tires before you get a flat." GB skillfully changed the subject. "Besides, I just bought fresh green beans and strawberries."

"But it's not that far out of the way. I can see it from here. Pleeeease?" I begged as we got on our bikes.

How could he refuse?

Boards covered the window panes at the front entrance of the Washington House where the robbers broke in the night before. Two policemen stood outside the door, looking over their notes.

"Jiminy!" GB sputtered as we walked up to the crime scene. To our surprise, the museum and ice cream parlor were still open for business.

"Please be careful." One of the officers reached for the door handle to help us inside.

It felt like I was stepping back in time to the late 1800s. Black-and-white pictures hung on the walls, small round tables stood in front of an old-fashioned saloon, and past-time relics were displayed everywhere.

I started to head straight for the ice cream, but GB wanted to take in the nostalgic atmosphere first. Passing from room to room we saw old military uniforms, a ballroom, replicas of a historic dentist and doctor office, a crafted dollhouse, and much more.

Nothing seemed out of place except for a few empty showcases as we entered the parlor. Behind the counter, a gray-haired, elderly woman with wire-rimmed glasses greeted us with a smile. "Welcome to the Washington House. Have you been here before?"

"No, but my grandson Dominic had a taste for some ice cream. We heard about the robbery. I'm surprised to see you're open so soon."

"Yes, it's all true and most untimely indeed." She frowned. "Two Rivers is holding a televised commemoration to celebrate the 130th anniversary of the ice cream sundae in just a few days. It's even drawn national attention due to a recently discovered ledger by Ed Berners' grand-nephew that would finally put an end to the sundae wars … before it was stolen, that is."

"I've never heard of sundae wars," I admitted.

"A few disputes developed over who created the first sundae, but only the city of Ithaca, New York continues to challenge our claim. They insist our stories are made-up, whereas they have a preserved sundae ad from 1892. As a result, a friendly rivalry has existed between the two communities ever since."

"So, the ledger must keep a record of sales for sundaes dated earlier than 1892?" GB pinned the tail on the donkey.

"Right you are. The *Ithaca Times* printed this in response to all of our recent publicity." She showed us the headline.

TWO RIVERS SUNDAE
CLAIM TO FAME WON'T FLOAT

"Anyway," the lady smiled at me, "what will it be? Did you decide?"

I relayed my order to her, eyes wide with anticipation. "I'll take the red, white, and blue special that comes with strawberries, blueberries, and chocolate syrup. I'd also like extra cream and a cherry on top. Hold the nuts, please."

"Alright, sir." She winked, then turned to Grandpa Bob. "And how about you, young man?"

"I'll take a dish of vanilla."

What? "Come on, GB. Ice cream sundaes were invented here." I raised my hands in the air. "You need to live a little." I pointed out all the different flavors of ice cream and toppings.

"I've never gone wrong with vanilla and I'm not about to push my luck."

The lady shrugged.

As we gobbled our ice cream, I scanned a few pictures hanging on the wall of Ed Berners and his parlor, until a framed document caught my attention. I examined it quickly while GB scraped the last bit of ice cream from the bottom of his dish.

RESOLUTION FORMALLY CHALLENGING THE CITY OF ITHACA, NEW YORK

Be it further resolved, that the city of Ithaca is hereby directed to cease and desist from its continued claims of being the "birthplace of the ice cream sundae," lest the city of Two Rivers be forced to take further action to set the historical record straight.

That didn't sound too friendly. Maybe the Two Rivers resolution backfired, refueling the "sundae wars" with Ithaca.

"Thanks for the ice cream," I said to the nice lady as we got up to leave. "Hope those crooks get what they deserve."

"I'm sure they're long gone by now, but if you see or hear anything suspicious, we'd appreciate it if you'd let us know before the broadcast."

We needed to put some air in my tires and pick up a few other things, so we made a quick pit-stop at the Mobil gas station before getting back on the trail.

While GB engaged himself in a long-winded conversation with the cashier about purchasing a can of WD-40 for the cranks on Nimrod, I decided to check out the candy aisle. As I reached for a bag of Skittles, a raspy, metallic voice on the other side of the rack caught my attention.

"There's been a delay so we'll have to lie low for a while. I'll let you know as soon as we've disposed of the evidence."

Huh. That sounded suspicious.

The man was bending down to get a newspaper, a cell phone pressed tightly to his cheek, with a wide-brimmed hat shadowing his face. The only thing I could make out was his mouth. As he finished talking, I caught a glimpse of a shiny gold tooth.

I wanted to get a closer look at him, so I followed as he exited the building. He made his way through the sliding doors and around a delivery truck. By the time I got to the other side he was gone.

I had an eerie feeling this guy was up to no good. Could he be one of the ice cream bandits?

CHAPTER 4

As our bikes wound down the dirt and gravel trail, I thought about the suspicious man with the gold tooth, the 130th commemoration ceremony, and the strange-but-true sundae wars between Two Rivers and Ithaca.

I couldn't wait to get to the campground to tell Forest and Sailor the news, but we didn't race this time; GB had a basket full of fresh produce and WD-40 to balance.

"Can I stop to see my friends when we get back?"

I thought GB would never say no, but he uttered a stern "no" anyway.

"Why not?"

"Because, you can't just go waltzing around someone else's campsite like that."

"Well, what if you came with me? Then you could ask their grandma if it's alright."

GB didn't present any objections, so we pedaled past the park entrance to the north and took the next left toward the group site. It loomed ahead, spread big enough for five Winnebagos.

Colorful tie-dye clothing hung across a laundry line that ran through the campground and over a caravan of tents below. A whale of a hammock stretched between two mammoth tamarack trees; dozens of wind catchers swaying overhead. We walked toward a screen tent which appeared to have … beads hanging in the doorway?

Something else seemed out of place, too—the ranger's truck. I was glad to have GB with me. Ranger Rick was talking to a man with a ponytail, taking notes on a pad. Ponytail's T-shirt had a crossed-out ice cream cone on it which reached to the middle of his cut-off jean shorts.

"Well, hello there. I'm Windsong."

I turned to see a barefoot woman with long, white braids walking toward us. She smiled as she reached her hand out to me. She looked like she belonged back in the 60s … a hippie, or maybe a gypsy. Well, let's just say she's a hipsy.

"Uh, hi. Um, are Forest and Sailor here?"

"Oh, you must be Dominic." As she turned to GB her smile widened, "And that would make you Grandpa Bob. Am I right?"

"Yes, you are," GB confirmed as they shook hands. "Looks like quite the shindig you have going on here."

"We reserve this site every year for a reunion of sorts, if you know what I mean."

"Oh, yes. I owned a few bell-bottom jeans in my day." GB gave a goofy laugh. "Though I'll admit they probably wouldn't fit anymore."

GB seemed captivated by Windsong, looking all groovy in her skirt and flowered top and all. If her braids weren't white I never would've guessed she was anyone's grandma.

"The kids left a little while ago to look for you. I think they mentioned a—" she glanced from me toward Ranger Rick and lowered her voice, "—secret fort."

27

Like clockwork, Ranger Rick jerked his head around. "What did you just say, Flower-top?"

"Oh, I asked if anyone would like a piece of … chocolate torte."

"I'd love some, but not right now. I have more interrogating to do."

"But Officer," Ponytail continued, "I just wanted to report that my clothes were stolen off the line. I swear I didn't take down any sundae flyers from your bulletin board."

"Well, someone did, and here you are with your 'Just-Say-No-to-the-Cone' shirt. What are you, some kind of nut?"

"You'd better run along now," Windsong whispered to me, as if she knew the problem I had with Ranger Rick. I felt an instant camaraderie with her.

GB gave me a nod that it was okay to leave. Turning to go, I heard him ask Windsong how she managed to walk around barefoot over all the pine needles and what-not. I looked back just as she showed him the bottoms of her feet. *Yuck!*

When I got back to our campsite, I saw two bikes parked in the grass next to the fire pit, so I headed over the hill to see if Forest and Sailor were in the fort.

"Dominic?" Sailor spied me, grabbed her purple-flowered flip-flops, and skipped in my direction. "We were hoping you'd get here soon. The bugs are eating us alive."

If you've never camped in Northern Wisconsin, you might not be familiar with the blood-sucking plague that torments us every summer—mosquitoes.

Forest waited in the fort, barefoot, jeans full of holes. He swatted a swarm of bugs with his baseball cap. "We came over here to avoid the commotion. Someone stole Jim's clothes off the laundry line."

"I already know, I just stopped by your place to look for you, and Ranger Rick was still there," I reported. "Not only that, but he accused your hippie friend of taking down ice cream flyers, besides."

"Jim's super nice, but he can sure be a weirdo." Sailor rolled her eyes.

"I wonder if any of it has something to do with

the Washington House burglary."

"Why do you say that?" Forest grumbled, still agitated from the mosquitoes.

"GB and I went there today. They keep a collection of artifacts, some of which were stolen last night, including a valuable old ledger that proves they invented the first ice cream sundae."

My wheels started spinning. "There's a big ceremony taking place in Two Rivers in just a few days. I think whoever stole the ledger wants the town to lose credibility and look like fools on national television."

Forest nudged my shoulder. "Hey, perfect time for you and your grandpa to pull up with your Nimrod."

"Very funny." I crossed my arms. "Besides all that, I overheard some creepy guy at the gas station talk about 'lying low' and 'disposing of evidence.' It seems like too much of a coincidence. I think the crooks might still be hanging around for some reason."

Forest and Sailor looked at each other and shrugged.

A grey, overcast sky loomed above; the waves

whipping onto the shore in a frenzy.

"It's getting pretty nasty out here. Do you guys want to start a campfire?" I asked. They both shook their heads, partly because they were shivering, so we climbed back over the sand ridge to my campsite.

Forest and Sailor settled into the circle of chairs neatly arranged around the fire pit. Thanks to GB, I quickly drew a supply of wood, packed Boy Scout-style, from his stash beneath Nimrod. I grabbed some of his homemade fire starters made of wax and straw in paper cups. The campfire roared to life in no time. Unfortunately, it didn't deter the mosquitoes.

"Geez," I smacked one that landed on my arm, "I swear these mosquitoes were waiting for us with forks and bibs."

"What's going on here?"

Surprise, surprise. Ranger Rick walked up the driveway to our campsite and stood there, hands on hips, just waiting for an explanation—for what, we had no idea.

"Oh, we're up to no good, Officer," Forest confessed. "We're having a campfire at a campground."

I wanted to give Forest a pat on the back, but that would come across as blasphemous, given the circumstances.

"I can see that, Illi-noyance. But you don't need to burn the place down." The smoke started curling in his direction. He put his hands out as if to stop it, wrinkling his nose at the billowing fumes.

Just then, the sky opened, and it started pouring. Ranger Rick scrambled back down the driveway—probably left his hat in the patrol truck and the downpour threatened to ruin his bouffant hairdo.

He called back over his shoulder, "If I see a fire like that again, I'll be writing a citation."

We dashed inside Nimrod for cover. So much for a campfire, but then again—so much for Ranger Rick. *And the Dominator reigns again.* Though I'm not sure how much credit I could take for the weather.

Dark clouds and rain didn't do Nimrod any favors. Even on a bright, sunny day it felt dark and ominous inside those canvas walls, but at least we stayed warm and dry—which is more than I could say for the mosquitoes.

"Do you guys want to play cards or dominos?" We could always count on one thing in GB's man cave—he kept it stocked with fun games and junk food. I set some snacks and soda on the table, dropping a stack of games alongside them.

"Hey, Dominic, what are these?" Sailor pushed the set of walkie-talkies toward me.

"GB and I use them to communicate with each other."

Forest laughed, which caused the big gulp of root beer he had just downed to come back up through his nose. "Are you kidding me, Dominic? Geez, first you have this rickety old camper and now walkie-talkies? Why don't you see if you can ring up Fred Flintstone on that thing?"

"For your information, Mr. Fancy Pants, the cell phone reception here is zilch. These walkie-talkies may look like relics to you, but at least they're reliable."

"Chillax, Dominic." Forest surrendered, putting

his hands up. "I get the point."

"You should talk! GB and I stopped at your campsite earlier today, and we met your grandma. She was dressed like a hippie."

Sailor cracked a smile. "Yep, that's Windsong, alright. She grew up in the '60s—went to Woodstock, hitch-hiked to San Francisco, wore flowers in her hair —all that stuff."

"Wow. I suppose it must be cool to have a grandma like that!" I wiped the orange residue from my lips and reached for another pile of cheese curls.

"Just for the record, don't ever call her 'Grandma.' It's Windsong, if you know what's good for you," Forest added. "Being called Grandma makes her feel old."

While the rain pierced tattoos on the roof, we played a good share of games and loaded up on some carbs. Suddenly, my walkie-talkies squawked to life, interrupting a serious game of Careers.

Kwwwttchh, "Coyote to Bigfoot, where you at?"

Kwwwttchh ... "Come in, Bigfoot."

"It's 'Sasquatch,' you idiot. Sasquatch. I'm at home base, Moron." *Kwwwttchh ...*

"That was weird." Sailor bent forward, eyes wide.

I jerked upright and froze like a popsicle. I'd heard that raspy voice before.

"Hey, guys, I swear that's the same man from the gas station. I'd recognize that voice anywhere. He's the one who calls himself 'Sasquatch.'"

"It sounded like he had a horse stuck in his throat," Forest noted.

"Well, they definitely seem sketchy, whoever they are," Sailor agreed. "What's a sasquatch, anyway?"

"Haven't you ever heard of Bigfoot?" Forest sighed. "You know—the big, hairy creeper of the north woods?"

Just then, the handle on the camper door started to wiggle. Someone outside was trying to get in. The door cracked slightly open, revealing a dark figure.

We didn't feel like playing games anymore.

CHAPTER 5

"Land sakes, it's pouring outside!" It was only GB. I exhaled in relief.

"Come on, kids. I'll give you a ride back so your grandma doesn't have to worry about you." Forest and Sailor made a mad dash for the truck.

That night it took forever to fall asleep. I had finally drifted off to la-la land when the morning sunlight bluntly roused me, its rays intruding through the rambling gaps of pine branches that canopied overhead.

It looked like the storm had lifted, and at least for the time being there was one less thing to worry about. But then again, the unresolved issues with Ranger Rick, the mysterious voice on my walkie-talkie, and the vampire mosquitoes, still lingered. Looks like I had my work cut out for me.

"Dominic, are you going to sleep the day away?"

GB bustled about in the kitchen as the smoky aroma of frying bacon filled up the camper. I was thrilled. Maybe that would help Nimrod's musty smell.

"Grandpa, please … just five more minutes." I buried my head under the blanket.

"Time to get up." GB cranked up his oldies radio station.

There ought to be a law against such rude awakenings, and with that, I rolled out of bed and onto the floor. The loud thud didn't seem to faze GB.

He started pounding the fried bacon with a big wad of paper towels, as though he'd cornered it in a boxing ring. The bacon looked positively limp.

Ding, ding, ding, ding. Ladies and gentlemen, we have a winner.

"What time is it?" I moaned.

"It's 9:00—time for the beach."

"Isn't it a little early for the beach?" I stretched and yawned.

"I have to make sure I get a good spot, so eat up."

I just couldn't picture the crowd being so large

that a person couldn't find an open spot, but that's GB for you. In the winter, he's outside with a shovel trying to catch every snowflake before it hits the ground.

"Grandpa, can I go for a bike ride after breakfast?" I wanted to see if anything mysterious happened at the campground overnight.

"As long as you don't take too long and meet me at the beach for lunch right after."

"Well, yeah. I have to eat, don't I?" *Am I the only one worrying about myself here?*

"Oh, and is it okay if I bring Forest and Sailor? We're sort of working on a project together." I wanted to tell him about the walkie-talkie incident, but he probably wouldn't believe me, anyway. He always said my imagination was working overtime.

"I could invite Windsong, too."

"That sounds like a great idea." GB seemed a little more interested now.

I wolfed down breakfast, then raced off on my bike. Taking a shortcut past a row of campers on my way to the group site, I searched for anything unusual.

Just past the shower building, an eye-catching bonanza on site #74 reminded me that it must be the same camp hosts I met last year.

Mr. and Mrs. Buckley covered their site with palm trees. Not real palm trees, mind you. The wire ones, all decorated in green lights. They must get Wisconsin confused with Florida, God love 'em.

Mom taught me that whenever people act strange, I should just say, "God love 'em."

I walked over to Bert Buckley, who was wiping off bugs from the front of his golf cart. He glanced up at me and shouted, "Well hello, young fellow!" Even though I stood right next to him, I doubt he realized how loud he was talking without his hearing aids in.

"Remember me? I'm Dominic." I parked my bike by a palm tree. Mr. Buckley's wife, Sadie, got up from her pink plastic chair and walked over to get a better look at me.

"Oh, yes. Aren't you Mitchell?"

She's the type that gets confused easily, so I had to repeat my name for her.

Just when I thought I cleared that up, Mr. Buckley asked, "Who are you, again?"

Sadie spoke into his good ear. "This is Dom-i-nic." Turning back to me, she whispered, "Bert doesn't hear very well anymore."

I didn't get why she felt the need to lower her voice after telling me he can't hear, but, oh well.

"It's nice to see young people camping these days." Mrs. Buckley smiled as she wiped her hands on her apron, briefly ruffling her grayish-blue curls.

"Yeah, I love camping … anyway, I was wondering if you've seen any suspicious activity around here lately?" I kept the conversation strictly business.

"Well, now, what sort of activity are you referring to?" Mr. Buckley stood up, stretching his hunched-over back.

"I mean, have you seen any shady characters hanging around?"

"So far, just you," Bert guffawed.

I rolled my eyes. Obviously I made a mistake in trying to get any help from these two. They seemed one sandwich short of a picnic.

Out of the corner of my eye, I saw Ranger Rick's truck approaching the campground. I quickly excused myself, hopped on my bike, and started toward the hipsy's campsite. Behind me, I heard Sadie scolding Bert for being rude.

Loose gravel spit and popped beneath my tires as I sped along the road. I ditched my bike behind some bushes to cover my tracks from Ranger Rick before heading into the Point Beach version of Woodstock.

A hippie guy with bushy eyebrows and tattoo-covered arms sang while strumming a guitar. I almost started whistling along … almost.

"Hey, Dominic." Sailor's head popped up from the hammock as she motioned me over.

A pine bough slapped me in the face as I headed in her direction. So much for looking dignified. "Where's Forest?"

"He's by the fire pit. Come on." She jumped out of the hammock. The first thing I noticed, other than her pigtails, was that her socks didn't match. I guess that made her Pippi "Wrong" Stocking. *The detective in me never missed a beat.*

"Um, did you know your socks don't match?"

"Yep, I know. This morning I couldn't decide on the red or the green socks, so I wore one of each."

She seemed oblivious as far as popular opinion in the fashion arena goes. I had to give her credit—she didn't seem to care what anyone thought about her. Me? I worried about popular opinions all the time.

I followed her to the fire pit where Forest sat, hanging out with a few long-haired hippies, eating peanuts and throwing the shells into the flames.

The guys would've looked normal if not for their tie-dye shirts and headbands, but the ladies looked even more out of this world. One had big, frizzy hair, and wore bell-bottoms with Birkenstocks. Windsong sat next to her, immersed in a weaving project.

"Hi Gran—Moon—um, Windsong." Dang, her name really threw me for a loop.

"Well, far out! It's Dominic." Windsong beamed. "Pull up a chair."

"My grandpa's grilling on the beach today." I sat down next to her. "Can Forest and Sailor come over? You can come too, if you're not too busy with whatever you're doing there."

"Groovy." Windsong looped some colorful threads together. "It's a great day to soak up the sun. I could even bring some of my famous tofu brownies."

"Cool," I replied half-heartedly. "Hey, Windsong, do you have any other relatives named after the place where they were born, like Forest and Sailor?"

Windsong's gaze clouded. "What on earth are you talking about?"

"So, they weren't born in the woods or on a boat?" A quick glance at Forest trying to cover his smirk confirmed my suspicion.

"You Scooby-Doo'ed me, didn't you Forest?" I stomped my foot.

Forest was laughing so hard he nearly fell off his chair. "Ruh-roe, Shaggy!"

Ugh. Why am I always so darn gullible?

"Aw, don't pay any attention, Dominic. My

43

grandkids were born in a hospital like regular folk." Windsong patted my leg.

She turned to Forest, wagging a finger at him. "Mister, you'd better check if your pants are on fire. What did I tell you about lying?"

Forest tried to stifle a chuckle. "Come on, Dominic. I was just having fun with you."

I jumped up from my chair and started walking away.

"I won't try to fool you again, I swear, Scout's honor." Forest held up two fingers—the wrong fingers, and there should've been three. Obviously, Forest was never a Boy Scout.

"Hey Jim, watch this." Sailor waved at the ponytail guy who'd been talking to Ranger Rick the day before. She proceeded to do a cartwheel, nearly landing in the fire.

"Outta sight!" Jim didn't seem fazed, but everyone else was a little on-edge by the near-accident. He wore black leather pants with a chain hanging from his belt loop. As he clapped, I noticed a tattoo that looked like a coyote on his right forearm.

Hmm ... what if he was one of the bad guys? This was as good a time as any to do some legwork on the case.

"So, Jim," I cleared my throat, "have you ever been to New York?"

"Yeah. I rode my motorcycle there for a concert once, back in the day."

Not quite what I was looking for. "Say, I noticed the shirt you had on yesterday. How come you don't like ice cream?"

"It's despicable!" Jim jumped up, clenching his fists. "Forcing cows to make milk all day is wrong. Animals should be treated fairly. They should live on the range where the deer and the antelope play."

I couldn't deny Jim's *utterly* passionate response, and quoting a kindergarten song was a nice touch.

"Don't worry about Jim." Windsong looked up from her weaving, "He avidly protests for animal rights. It's a sore subject."

I would've indulged in the hippie life a bit longer,

but after that conversation, it appeared I had work to do.

"Come on, guys. Are you ready to go?" I wanted to get to the fort.

"Sure." Sailor ran toward her tent. "I just have to change into shorts, first."

"You might want to change your socks while you're at it," Forest teased, which sent Sailor foraging for her flip-flops.

I proceeded to the bushes where I fished out my bike and walked it toward the road. I started to formulate a plan in my mind while I waited for the others to join the cavalry.

Unfortunately, just as Forest and Sailor pulled alongside me on their bikes, Ranger Rick slowly cruised by in his work truck. "Well, if it ain't Illi-noyance and Illi-nuisance."

I really didn't like that guy. We all just stood there, staring. I found myself tongue-tied, floundering for something, anything at all to say, until quick-witted Forest saved the day.

"D-N-R?" He pointed at the emblem on the ranger's truck. "Does that stand for 'Department of Nasty Rangers,' or what?" Forest ran a hand through his hair, offering a lopsided grin. Sailor held up her hand to high-five him.

Ranger Rick glowered at them, shoved his sunglasses back up his nose and drove off. Out of the corner of my eye, I noticed him pick up something from off the dash.

Did I imagine it, or was he holding a walkie-talkie in his hand?

As we made our way to the fort, my thoughts turned to Ranger Rick. I wondered if he could be hiding two crooks at the campground, or maybe Jim was really Coyote, trying to throw Ranger Rick off his scent by reporting his clothes stolen, not to mention his tattoo and lactose intolerance.

Something suspicious was going on at Point Beach, and I remained determined to figure it out.

CHAPTER 6

The blazing sun hovered in the July sky with throngs of people packing the beach to the gills. Maybe GB hadn't completely lost his marbles by getting here early.

Kids were building sandcastles and brightly colored kites twirled over the lake, tempting me to forget the business at hand and go have some serious fun. Sitting still seemed particularly challenging for Sailor, who was twisting her pigtails into tightly-woven circles ever since we'd arrived at the fort.

Forest turned his attention from the lake back to me. "So, let me get this straight, Dominic. You think someone camping in this park broke into the museum and stole the ledger? And you think we're going to nab them and solve some big mystery? What are we, Nancy Drew and the Hardy Boys?"

"Look, I'm telling you, the voice I heard downtown was the same one on my walkie-talkie, which only has a one-to-two-mile range. That means those guys had to be nearby when we picked up the signal."

Forest rubbed the back of his neck. "Even if the crooks are here at the campground, we have absolutely nothing to go on. No description of the suspects or the getaway vehicle."

"Wait …" I started to remember. "The guy at the gas station was trying to conceal himself, but I noticed he had a gold tooth."

"Well, that helps a lot," he said.

"Okay, so we don't have all the pieces of the puzzle just yet, but what we *do* have is two suspicious characters who call themselves 'Coyote' and 'Sasquatch,' who are nearby, and seem to be hiding something. How many grown men do you know who use code names?"

"Dominic's right. If you think about it, a campground is the perfect hideout." Sailor kicked off her flip-flops, crossing her legs, pretzel-style. "I mean, who's gonna find them? Ranger Rick?"

"Maybe he's in on it," Forest added. "It would explain why he's been acting all jumpy and paranoid."

"Ranger Rick is a little out there, but that doesn't make him a criminal," Sailor insisted.

"Maybe not, but what kind of ranger doesn't like the outdoors?" I cracked open an Orange Crush, taking a swig. "The guy's a neat-freak. He runs for cover when it rains and he hates getting dirty."

"Yeah … maybe he doesn't like his job and is looking for a way out." Forest scratched his head.

"I think we have one more suspect in play. How well do you guys know this Jim character?"

Sailor crossed her arms. "Come on, Dominic. Now you suspect Jim?"

"He has a coyote tattoo," I argued, but Sailor stood her ground.

"It looks more like a wolf to me. Besides, he's a good friend of Windsong's. She's known him for years, and I think if he was a criminal, we'd know about it."

"We can't rule anyone out." Forest turned to me. "So what do you suppose we do about it?"

At least he was taking me seriously now. Then again, with Forest it was hard to tell.

"I'll think of something, but first, let's go look for GB on the beach. I'm starving." *Sometimes my stomach calls the shots. What can you do?*

As we scrambled down the sand dune, I scanned the coastline for a balding, silver-haired man with metal tongs in his hand. If that didn't get me there, I'd follow my nose. GB didn't grill just anything—it was Johnsonville brats or nothing.

Lake Michigan's waves washed onto the cinnamon sand shore. A handful of seagulls floated above beach umbrellas while another group of daring gulls attacked an unopened bag of potato chips abandoned on a teal-striped beach towel.

"Hey Dom, over here." GB waved from behind the smoking grill.

"What's that?" I never should've asked.

"Veggie burgers. Try one."

"Where's the brats?"

GB gave me the *look* when Windsong walked

over. She breathed deeply. "Oh, Bobby, your cooking smells dynamite."

Whatever that's supposed to mean?

"Yeah, great." I tried to remain a good sport even though everything about this picnic made me gag.

Windsong smiled and headed to a table planted under a shade tree. Sailor joined her, but Forest stuck around to take grilling pointers from GB.

"How do you flip them like that?" Forest seemed amazed by how a patty could fly a foot in the air and not fall on the ground.

GB liked nothing better than being complemented on his cooking skills. I was more interested in searching for some cookies so I wouldn't starve to death.

"Say, did you see there's more in today's paper about the Two Rivers robbery?" Windsong called over to GB as I approached the picnic table. Forest and Sailor scrambled over.

"Now they're offering a reward for any information leading to an arrest, and boy, it's a dandy."

My chin nearly dropped to the dirt.

ROBBERY UPDATE À LA MODE

Police are looking for information involving a robbery at the Historic Washington House, located at 1622 Jefferson Street in Two Rivers. Images taken by surveillance cameras showed two masked men forcefully entering the building at approximately 3:30am on Wednesday, July 10th. One suspect carried a blue laundry bag.

The estimated value of losses and damages for vandalism of the building, a stolen cash box, and many missing museum artifacts including a priceless ledger are staggering. The suspects remain at large.

Anyone with information leading to the arrest or conviction of the persons responsible for this robbery may be eligible to receive up to a $30,000 cash reward through Crime Stoppers.

Call (920) 683-4466 with information. You may remain anonymous.

Our grandparents were clueless about our interest in the thefts. If only they knew we had a pretty good idea where the crooks were hiding—somewhere very close to Point Beach.

CHAPTER 7

We let the newest information about the robbery settle, along with our lunch. The veggie burgers didn't taste half-bad. If you loaded them with ketchup and mustard, you could barely tell they were good for you.

"Hey kids, would you like to go with us to Door County for some cherries and cheese?" GB asked.

Did we want to go with them … did we want to go with them … No. With GB and Windsong out of our hair, we could get started on our mission in the campground.

"No thanks. We're going to build a sandcastle … or something."

See what a bad influence Forest was on me?

"Alright, but stay out of the lake while we're gone. If you get into trouble, head for the camp host site," Windsong instructed. A flashback of blue-haired

Sadie Buckley gave me the willies.

The two of them began packing up the picnic while we made our way back to the fort.

"Did you see the amount of that reward?" Sailor started skipping excitedly.

"Let's not get ahead of ourselves." I pretended not to feel the same way. "We need to keep our eyes and ears open for more clues or anything out of the ordinary that might lead us to Sasquatch and Coyote."

"We should ask the camp hosts," Sailor suggested. "If anyone would catch on to things like that, it would be them."

"I already talked to them and they didn't know much, but it wouldn't hurt to ask again," I said.

"I have a better idea—let's ask Ranger Rick." Forest tossed a corn nut into the air, opened his mouth to catch it, and watched it drop onto the sand at his feet.

"Yeah. Ranger Rick will save the day, and my bike will take me to the moon and back. Come on, guys. Let's get serious." Then an idea hit me, or maybe it was just a corn nut. "We can use the campground map and start by ruling out families with children and elderly people to narrow down the suspect list."

Forest and Sailor agreed.

When we got back to the campsite, I wasted no time in grabbing the map, camera, and walkie-talkies. "GB and Windsong will be gone for a while, so we can use Nimrod as home base while we investigate."

"Do we have to call it Nimrod?" Forest whined. "It sort of cheapens the whole deal."

"I like it." Sailor hopped onto her flowered banana-seat bike. "It's old-school."

"Fine. We won't call it anything, okay?" I started to wonder if I should just try to solve this mystery by myself. "Let's start with some spy work. We can look for New York license plates and take pictures of anyone who looks suspicious." I strapped on my backpack and straddled my bike. "It's go-time!"

As we coasted past the camp host site, Sadie tried to get my attention; yellow gloves up to her elbows, a pile of poison ivy beside her.

"Martin! Yoo-hoo, Martin!"

Ughhh ... will she ever get my name right? I used my sneakers as brakes, swerving in her direction.

"Hey guys, hold up!" I yelled to Forest and Sailor. They collided into each other behind me.

"Who do we have here?" She carefully removed her gloves.

"These are my friends, Forest and Sailor."

"Well, now, those are some names you don't hear every day."

Bert came walking over. "Who is this, Dear?"

"For-est and Sail-or."

"Oh, Forest and Sailor. Huh. Those are names you don't hear every day."

Sometimes I think Sadie and Bert were shooting from the same gun.

"It's a long story, Sir." Forest left it at that.

"Well, I have news for you." Sadie walked over to a fake palm tree, brushing the dirt from her knees. "Martin, remember how you asked if we noticed any suspicious strangers around here?"

I nodded while anxiously trying to keep my mind

from running away at the possibilities.

"Yesterday I was taking Sprinkles for a walk," she stooped down, tousling her poodle's curls, "and we saw a stranger. Didn't we, my little love muffin? Oh yesh, my wittle baby, yesh we did."

Ughhh ... I slowly released my pent-up breath between my teeth. "Okay, so then what happened?" I was getting impatient.

Sailor, on the other hand, seemed to be captivated. A smile played on her lips as she stared at Sadie in the same way a person would stare at a cute puppy.

"He was talking on one of them gadgets, but when he saw us coming he lowered his voice."

My heart skipped a beat. "And what did he say?"

"Well, now, I don't know. He was whispering, so I couldn't quite make it out." Sadie stroked her chin.

"What did he look like?"

"He was wearing sunglasses ... and a hat."

She seemed quite pleased with herself. Unfortunately, none of that helped.

"So, you really don't know anything?"

"No. I guess not."

And with that, the three of us hit the road.

"*Shhh*, Sailor," I hissed. She kept blathering about the color of her nail polish. "This is a stakeout. Keep it down."

We crouched behind a row of bushes, along with some mosquitoes, and pointed the camera at site #83. This Mom-and-Pop crew appeared to be harmless.

"Tommy, stop wallopin' yah sistah with that fly swattah," someone shouted.

A mischievous boy with freckles and green eyes chased a girl about the same age around the campsite. She managed to stay just out of his reach.

Holy cow, what planet were these campers from? I managed to stifle a chuckle, but Forest? Not so much. A low belly-laugh emitted from his direction. I shot him a brisk, "*Shhh*," hoping we could develop a more serious attitude.

"Momma! Tommy won't stop swattin' at me. I'm trahn to put this caterpillah in a jah!"

I narrowed the tribe's origin down to Boston, by the Massachusetts plates on their brand-spanking-new Winnebago. Close to New York, but not quite.

"Okay, mistah smahty pants." Mom grabbed Tommy by the nape of his neck, towing him to the rear door of the RV.

The only crime this family committed was that they were clearly first-time campers. We needed to move on. We backed up from the bushes, snorting all the while in our attempts to hold back our laughter and maintain our cloak-and-dagger routine.

All fun aside, by the end of the day I felt let-down. Most of the RV sites lacked any signs of life; probably due to the sunny weather. More than likely everyone was either hiking, biking, or at the beach. Of the few campers we did observe, none of them seemed like the stealing type.

Even though we hadn't inspected the tent sites yet, we needed a break. Nothing helps clear your mind like something cold and refreshing, so we made our way to the camp store. It was a good thing Mom gave me some "emergency" cash to take along.

While Sailor and I licked our ice cream cones, Forest took one last slurp of his slushy. "Well, Dominic, so far this was a big waste of time, just like I said to begin with." He stretched his hands behind his head and yawned. "We should've stayed at the beach."

Maybe I was way off with this whole theory. My sixth sense seemed to be out of order. Embarrassment crept up my cheeks. Maybe Forest was ri—

Kwwwttchh … "Come in, Coyote."

It came from inside my backpack. I yanked out my walkie-talkie.

"Coyote, here. What's your twenty? That's police lingo for 'what's your location.'"

"I'm well aware of the code, you idiot. Stop playing cops and robbers. Have you disposed of the … *items* yet?"

"Ah, that's a big ten-four, Sasquatch."

"Good work, Coyote. Now we wait for Badger so

we can finish our mission and get out of here."

"Right, Sasquatch. Over and off. Over and done. Uh, over and out."

I leveled my victorious gaze at Forest. *Well, how do you like me now?*

CHAPTER 8

Worry lines spread across Sailor's forehead. "From the sounds of it, Sasquatch and Coyote were trying to get rid of something. I hope it wasn't the ice cream store stuff."

"Well, if they were trying to get rid of their brains, it's too late," Forest teased. "Those two are the real nimrods."

"I don't think it's just 'two' anymore." I folded my map, tossing it in my backpack. "There must be a third accomplice called 'Badger' on the way. It seems like we're running out of time."

We hurried to home base in order to discuss our next plan of attack, but the investigation would have to wait for the time being. GB beat us back to camp. He was unloading shopping bags from the truck.

"What did you kids do all day?"

Forest and Sailor looked at each other and then at me without saying a word.

"Oh, nothing much. We did some hiking and sightseeing." Even if I had the guts to tell him what we actually did, I knew he'd put the kibosh on the whole operation.

"We ate some ice cream, too." Sailor licked her lips and smiled at Grandpa Bob.

"Sounds nice. Well, Windsong wanted to take a nap, but you're welcome to stay for pudgy pies." GB handed Forest a Ziploc bag. "Here, have some cheese curds while I make a fire."

"What's a cheese curd?" Sailor asked.

You gotta be kidding me. She really doesn't know what a cheese curd is? Poor, simple-minded Sailor. God love 'er.

"See for yourself." Forest popped a curd into his mouth and grinned. "Hey, these are squeaky. Try one."

She started to chew on one but quickly spit it out. "*Yuck.* Why is it squeaky? I don't like it."

I had to laugh at the look on her face. She wrinkled her nose like she had just bitten into a sour pickle.

Night descended over the campground, and after eating way too many pudgy pies, we took turns telling ghost stories around the fire. That got me thinking. I snuck inside Nimrod, grabbing the flashlights, walkie-talkies, and bug spray.

"What are you doing?" Forest noticed my loaded backpack.

"Night time is usually when the bad guys come out, right?"

Forest nodded.

"So, if we try investigating now, we may have more luck finding them ... as long as GB lets us go, that is."

"I might have an idea." Forest rubbed his chin for a moment. "Hey, Grandpa Bob, did you ever play night games when you were a kid, like ghosts in the grave-yard, and stuff like that?"

"I sure did. My brothers and sisters and I liked to go outside most summer evenings." He tilted his head back, reminiscing. "Night time was *fun* time."

"That's great, because Sailor and I want to teach Dominic how to play flashlight tag. Can we show him on our way back to our campsite?"

"Well, I'm not sure …"

I twisted his arm. "Pleeease—I never had a chance to play night games before. I've been deprived!"

"Are you sure you won't be scared out there in the dark?"

"We're sure," we promised.

"Alright, Dominic. Just don't take too long getting back, and don't talk to strangers."

"Don't worry, GB. We'll take the walkie-talkies along." I gave him a hug. "Thanks."

At least he didn't say I couldn't *look* for strangers. We crept out of the site, flashlight beams chasing each other with an occasional "Gotcha!" signaling that someone was tagged.

"I have the feeling you two are up to something," Sailor said after we regrouped. "What's going on?"

"I'm trying to think like a thief doing his dirty work under the cover of nightfall."

She chuckled. "You never give up, do you?"

The campground still boomed with life and glowed with light. A crook would need to go somewhere more private, somewhere like—"There!" I pointed at Ridges Trail which ran between the campsites.

It would make a perfect path for leading someone out to seclusion and secrecy. "Come on, guys. I have a hunch that Sasquatch and Coyote might be off in the woods somewhere, planning their next move."

The crickets created a symphony of sounds sure to camouflage the twigs crunching beneath our feet and the occasional slapping of mosquitoes. I only hoped they drowned out the random melodies Sailor kept humming as we made clumsy attempts to find our way deeper into the blackness.

I stopped for a moment. The eerie hooting of an owl echoed through the woods. "Hoo-hoo-too-hoo …"

"An owl! I love owls!" Sailor cheered.

So much for our covert operation. "Sailor—dang it! Keep it down."

"Oh, so what, Dominic. We're camping. Lots of

people are hooting and hollering this time of night." Forest made a good point.

I sighed. "Sorry, Sailor. Yes, it appears to be an owl. Can we move on now?"

"Nooooo. I want to see the owl. Do you think we can find it?" She scampered into the woods. "Hurry— it's getting away!"

We had no choice but to follow—not an easy task in the dark. Tree branches whipped our faces as we carved our way through the dense forest. Our flash- lights shed light no faster than our feet could carry us.

"HOO-HOO-TOO-HOO ..." Sailor ran in the di- rection of the last hoot with Forest and me lagging be- hind. "Hoo-hoo-too-hoo ..." The call sounded from fur- ther away. We followed the owl for what seemed like forever, until eventually we ran out of hoots.

"Nice going, Sailor. Now we're lost in the middle of the woods," Forest snapped.

"I just really wanted to see the owl." Sailor low- ered her head.

"Yeah, that was a real hoot." My legs began tingling all over. "Hey, I'm itchy."

Sailor started to look for the trail, but stopped at the sight of me scratching and started doing some scratching of her own. "What on earth? My legs itch like crazy, too."

I couldn't believe our bad luck. "Don't you see what's going on? We stepped in poison ivy!"

"I'm beginning to think taking a shortcut through the woods was a 'rash' decision," Forest teased.

I was in too much agony to laugh.

"Well, at least we're not lost, after all." Forest shined his flashlight around. The beam landed on a road sign for the group site. "That wild goose chase brought us right to our campsite. I'm going back."

"Will you be alright on your own, Dominic?" Sailor bit the inside of her cheek.

"Should be, but take this along in case something happens." I handed Forest one of the walkie-talkies, before they disappeared in the opposite direction.

I didn't want to give up the search, but I couldn't take much more of the itchiness, and now that I was alone, the woods seemed creepier. Anything could be out there … maybe even wolves.

Backtracking toward the sound of camping civilization, I rotated my flashlight back and forth in front of me, careful not to step in any more poison ivy. Suddenly, the beam caught a pair of glowing, green eyes staring right at me.

I screamed. My heart pounded. *Stay calm, and don't move.*

The creature scurried behind a wide, half-dead tree. *Phew. Probably just a squirrel.*

It seemed pretty small, but I scanned my flashlight up and down the trunk as a precaution. Light glinted off something like a cord, or a rope protruding from a rotted hole near the top.

I wanted to get a closer look, so I hugged the tree with my legs and arms, slowly hoisting my body upward, using notches and holes to get a good grip. Once I had climbed high enough, I bent one arm into the opening and felt around for the rope, hoping the furry creature wouldn't be there.

To my surprise, there was something soft, shoved deep inside the hollow. I reached in farther to dislodge it, but lost balance and tumbled backward. A protruding branch jabbed my side before I landed with a thud on the ground.

CHAPTER 9

Moaning in pain, I struggled to get back on my feet. I clutched my side with one hand and tried to turn on my flashlight with the other, but my fall had knocked it out.

From what I could tell, the new discovery was just a cloth sack with a bunch of clothes in it. I slung the mysterious bag over my shoulder and kept going. At least I wouldn't return to the campsite empty-handed.

Eventually, the tree covering parted, and the moon illuminated Ridges Trail. From there I found my way back to my site.

Campfire embers still glowed in the fire pit, but GB had retired inside, sawing logs in his sleep. I deposited the sack inside the fort for safekeeping, grabbed the calamine lotion and called it a night. *Stupid owl.*

I woke up the next morning feeling a bit groggy, and no wonder—I had nightmares all night about chasing an owl through the woods with Forest and Sailor. We ran after it like a bunch of fools until we got lost.

Oh, wait. That wasn't a dream.

Then I remembered the bag. GB was still sleeping, so I had a little time to check things out. I put on my sneakers and crept outside. It was right where I left it inside the fort. I opened the bag, pulling out two grey t-shirts and a pair of jeans. Then came something black, and something else that was black.

Whoa ... what do we have here? Two ski masks.

This must be *the* blue bag used in the robbery, even though it was more of a baby-blue with a dirty tree trunk tinge. I just knew it.

I dug deeper to see if some money, or even the ledger might be inside. I could hardly contain myself. I reached in, removing a handful of ... *underwear?* Gross! I stuffed everything back in the bag and ran for the hand sanitizer.

A million thoughts circled around in my head.

Well, maybe not a million, but if this constituted evidence from the crime scene, shouldn't I turn it in to the police? Or at least Ranger Rick? What about showing it to GB, or Windsong and her hippie friends, or the camp hosts?

The other option was to handle this quietly by ourselves until we could identify the crooks. Since we didn't rule out Ranger Rick as a suspect, I decided to wait until I could talk to Forest and Sailor. I pulled out my walkie-talkie.

"Dominator to Woody. Come in." I was Dominator, and Forest was Woody. We thought it might be too dangerous to use our real names in case the crooks were listening in.

I waited a few seconds, then heard the familiar *kwwwttchh*. "Woody, here. Go ahead, Dominator."

"There's an emergency. Meet me at home base."

"Will do."

When Forest and Sailor reached my campsite, I motioned quietly for them to follow me, leading them over the sand dune and onto the beach. "Stay here. I have to show you something."

I hauled the blue bag out of the fort and into the clearing. They just stared at me.

"A bag. Interesting." Forest failed to see the bigger picture.

"No, wait 'til you see this." I began to dump the contents at their feet. Unfortunately, the underwear fell out first.

"Yuck. Is that … underwear?" Sailor gagged.

"Nice," said Forest. "Fruit of the Loom."

With a groan, I fished out the black ski masks.

"Wait a minute." Forest squinted at me. "Is this *the* blue bag? The one from the ice cream shop heist?"

I nodded.

Sailor blinked a few times. "Does that mean the crooks are walking around naked?"

"No, more like they didn't want to be recognized from the surveillance camera footage," I suggested.

"I say we hand it over to Ranger Rick. Case closed." Forest seemed to want our mystery-solving days to be over, but I didn't want to give up so easily.

"Without knowing the true identity of the suspects, I don't think we should trust anyone, just yet."

"And why is this our problem? It's not like they stole anything special—just some ice cream store junk."

"Come on, Forest," Sailor said. "The whole city of Two Rivers thinks it's valuable. This is our chance to do something good for someone else."

"It's not in my nature to care about anyone."

"You need to get over yourself." Sailor clenched her fists.

I didn't know what to say anymore. Forest was in a funk, and I couldn't do much about it. As the three of us stood there, stewing, I realized I had to break from the pack.

"Fine. I'll finish this thing by myself." I grabbed the blue bag, shoved everything back inside, and began to scuffle up the dune. As soon as I turned my back on my friends, I faced an even bigger problem.

"What's in the bag, Nimrod?" A familiar, unpleasant voice broke the silence.

Busted.

CHAPTER 10

"You heard me." Ranger Rick stood atop the ridge, binoculars in hand. "What are you doing with that bag?"

In a panic, I tried to hide it behind my back. Unsure of what to do next, I turned to Forest with a look of dread on my face.

"It's just some dirty underwear in there, sir," Forest replied.

What! Couldn't he come up with something better than that?

Ranger Rick wasn't buying it. "What are you carrying around your dirty underwear for?" He turned toward me, but I remained speechless.

"Oh, it's not *his* underwear, Sir. I found it on the beach." As crafty as Forest could be, I doubted even he could pull this one off.

Ranger Rick's eyes ping-ponged between us. "I don't understand. You found a laundry bag on the beach, and just decide to make Nimrod carry it around for you?"

"Uh, yes sir ..." Forest said. "You see, I'm a kleptomaniac. Sometimes it gets bad, and then I have to take something for it. Dominic was just putting it back for me."

"Very funny. Well, you'd better hand it over," Ranger Rick demanded.

I hesitated. If he took the bag, we'd have no proof of anything.

Luckily, GB must've heard the ruckus. He hobbled over in his Green Bay Packer sweat suit. "What kind of three-ring circus is going on here? Dominic, is everything alright?"

"Excuse me," Ranger Rick shot a glare his way, "you can keep your cheese-head out of this."

"Excuse *me*," GB fired back. "Do you have something against the Packers?"

"No, I'm just more of a Badger fan," the ranger

squared off. "Now, if you don't mind, I'm trying to make sure your grandson and his side-kicks stay out of trouble for more than five minutes."

"Well, it sounds to me like you have bigger fish to fry." GB pointed in the direction of the ranger's vehicle.

Kwwwwich. "Come in, DNR247," resounded from the open window.

"Don't think for a minute that I don't know what you kids are up to." Ranger Rick pointed two fingers to his eyes and then the same two fingers back at us. "Nothing that happens at Point Beach gets past me."

He wheeled around, hurrying off toward his truck. *A Badger fan ... hmmm.*

"That ranger is quite the character." GB shook his head as he made his way back to the camper. "Come on down. Breakfast is served."

We all breathed a sigh of relief. That was almost a complete disaster. Forest walked over and patted me on the back. "I'm sorry if I sounded unfriendly before."

"Not compared to Ranger Rick," I said. "Thanks

for not throwing me under the bus when you had the chance, but did you have to say *dirty underwear*?"

"What are friends for?" Forest gave me another slug. "You know I'm not supposed to tell lies anymore."

"I'm glad the snot-slinging is over. It's nice to see you guys kiss and make-up." Sailor's eyes got all squinty whenever she tried to hold back a smile.

"Well, now that we have that settled, who else is hungry?" I deposited the blue bag in the fort and trudged back through the sand to good old Nimrod. Forest and Sailor were right behind me as I opened the door and walked into a strange, nauseating odor— something far worse than Nimrod's usual musty smell.

"Did something die in here?" My nose wrinkled.

"Nooooo. We're having pancakes and Spam for breakfast." GB had the meat cornered with a metal spatula. "You'll like Spam. It's the miracle meat."

I think he meant "mystery" meat. "Come on, Grandpa, can't we just have some Cheerios?"

GB lowered his brow, which was not a good sign.

We might as well give in. If I didn't eat soon, things could get ugly.

"Yeah, ummm, I think Windsong's calling us." Forest and Sailor slowly backed up. "Catch ya later."

"You know, Spam is considered a delicacy in Hawaii," GB called after them.

As soon as I finished the "delicacy," I grabbed my backpack, making a quick break for it while GB cleaned up.

We met up outside the shower building. Two little kids squealed while their mom tried to rinse the sand off their feet.

"Don't you think we're in over our heads and need some help?" Sailor chewed her fingernails.

"Let's give it to the end of the day," I reasoned. "Taking out the big guns might scare off the bad guys."

I reached for my handy campsite map. "We already covered the south end of the campground. Of course, not all the campers were at their sites, but I think we should move on to the tent-only section. I have a feeling these guys are keeping to themselves."

"Sounds good." Sailor smacked her peppermint gum. "Wouldn't it be cool if we caught the thieves and became famous?"

"Wipe the stars from your eyes, Sailor." Forest tugged on her ponytail. "We're probably just wasting our time again."

Good old Forest, always optimistic.

Sadie and Bert came our way, walking Sprinkles on a short leash. I wondered if they had any news since Mrs. Buckley said she'd keep an eye out. On the other hand, they might just tie us up by going on about how "cutsie" their "poopsie" was.

I wanted to get out of there, but it was too late. We had already made eye contact.

"Martin? Martin?" Sadie flagged me down.

Oh, brother. I could hardly wait.

Forest looked at me, confused.

"Never mind," I lamented. "It's a lost cause."

"Martin, I thought of something else about that strange man I saw the other day." Sadie ambled over before I could get away. "When he smiled, I noticed a blinding light coming from his mouth." She pointed to her own tooth to indicate the incisor she was referring to. "He had a gold tooth."

"A blinding light coming from his mouth … I don't know what that means." Bert squinted.

"It means you haven't taken your pill today, dear." Sadie patted his head in the same way she patted her poodle.

Interesting. "Where did you see him, again?"

"Down the road past the tent sites."

"Thanks for the info!"

We were just about to leave the shower building when Ranger Rick pulled into the camp host site directly across from us.

"Get down!" I ducked behind a fence, motioning them to follow suit.

"I don't think he saw us," Forest whispered. "We should be okay."

.

We watched as Ranger Rick tried to keep Sprinkles at bay. She kept barking and biting at his ankles while he talked to the Buckleys, creating the perfect diversion.

I led the way through the campground to the tent-only section. It seemed more primitive to be in a tent without electricity—certainly a good way to maintain a low profile. "Keep your eyes open and pay special attention to the campsites with fires burning. It's a good indication the occupants are still around."

While I searched each site for clues, Sailor got distracted by a hopscotch grid on the road. She hopped from one foot to two over the colored chalk squares until Forest gave her a shove that toppled her off-balance.

"Forest!" Sailor fell to the ground, shooting him an angry glare. Forest grinned impishly and kept on walking.

Great. Here we go again.

"Hey!" A scruffy man came into view. We gawked at him as he came closer.

He looked like a rat. Thinning salt-and-pepper

hair, a gaunt face covered in stubble, eyes set too far apart. His black leather pants hung on his waist, gangster-style. "Why don't you kids go play somewhere else?" His scratchy voice and flinty eyes sent a chill up my spine.

"Sorry, Mister." Sailor stood up, rubbing her skinned knee.

The man gave a fake smile, hoisting up his pants before disappearing behind an old, rusty brown van parked on site #42.

"Did you see that?" Forest said under his breath. "A gold tooth!"

CHAPTER 11

"That hillbilly gives me the creeps." Sailor shivered, quickening her pace. "I'm sure glad his pants didn't fall down. Does he have any idea what a belt is for? Gross."

I turned to face her, placing my hands on her shoulders. "You saw the gold tooth, didn't you, Sailor?"

Her eyes grew big as saucers. "You mean—that was Sasquatch?"

"In the flesh," Forest said. "Remember, Jim's clothes went missing? That ratty dude had on a paisley shirt, and Jim owns about a hundred of them. The crooks probably needed something to wear so they wouldn't be identified."

"Great detective work, Forest." Even I didn't catch on to that.

"So what do we do now?" Sailor held her arms tightly around her waist.

Suddenly the light bulb guy did a cartwheel in my head. "I bet they're hiding the goods in the van. If I can distract Sasquatch and get him away from the campsite, then Forest can check things out while you keep watch."

Sailor bit her lip. "No way, Dominic. It's too dangerous."

"Listen, Sailor, everything's going to be fine. Sasquatch won't catch me because his pants will probably end up around his ankles, and with you making sure the coast is clear for Forest, it'll be a cake-walk."

"I can go by myself. I don't need a babysitter," Forest insisted. But I knew better—the soft side of him wanted to protect his sister. Even though he had no problem bullying her, he'd never put her in harm's way.

"No, Forest. I can do it." Sailor exhaled a long breath. "But let's make it quick before I change my mind."

"Okay, then here's what we do." I pointed to

Ridges Trail on the map. "I'll enter site #42 from behind, get Sasquatch's attention, and take a picture with my camera as evidence. Then I'll lure him away from the van by heading back through the woods."

I pointed to the bathroom building. "You two stay under cover over here until I give the signal that Sasquatch took the bait. Forest, do you still have the walkie-talkie?"

"Yep." He slid it out of his pocket.

"Great—then we initiate phase two. Sailor, while Forest inspects the van for the artifacts, you patrol the road. If anything seems off, alert him with a 'hoot.' Either way, we'll meet up in Florida."

"Florida?"

"Yeah, you know. The palm tree people—Bert and Sadie."

"What about Ranger Rick?" Sailor asked.

"I'll think of something, but for now let's just stick with the plan."

"Got it." Forest nodded as he and Sailor turned to get into position while I headed off to Ridges Trail. I could feel my nerves begin to set in, but there was no turning back now. I hoped my instincts were right.

I weaved through the trees and across a swampy area that bordered the tent sites. Once I got close enough to site #42, I found a dense shrub to hide behind while I waited to make my move. I already had poison ivy, so I had nothing to lose.

Sasquatch stood there, tossing some sticks into the fire pit, totally unaware of me behind him. My palms began to sweat as I pulled the camera from my back pocket. I looked to the ground, locating a nice-sized rock, picked it up, and chucked it.

Bullseye.

Clunk. The rock struck the back of the van, adding another dent to its collection.

Sasquatch wheeled around. I held up the camera and yelled, "Say cheese!"

Click.

He glared at me as I shoved the camera back in my pocket. "Why, you little runt! I'm gonna make minced onions out of you!"

His reaction stunned me at first, but when I finally realized he was coming after me, I shouted, "Heading to Florida!" into the walkie-talkie. It was time to begin phase two.

"Hey, kid!" His razorblade voice gave me goose bumps. "Fat chance making it to Florida. You'll never make it out of the campground!"

I bolted. Leaves and sticks crackled beneath his feet letting me know he wasn't far behind. The walkie-talkie almost slipped from my sweaty grasp as I tried to run faster, but it didn't matter now. I was on my own.

My legs wobbled like jelly as I crossed the marshy ravine. I darted up the other side, burst through the trees and brush, and landed back onto Ridges Trail.

Just a little farther.

"Get back here, kid!" His angry shouts echoed through the woods as I raced toward the road.

Faster. Gotta run faster. I could hear his feet pounding on the pavement behind me, too close for comfort.

Up ahead I spotted Ranger Rick's truck still

parked by the camp host site. Sasquatch must've noticed it too. He slowed down and dropped back.

I never thought I'd be so deliriously happy to see Ranger Rick.

"Whoa! Slow down, Nimrod. What's the rush?"

I collapsed on the ground right in front of him. "I'm being chased by Sasquatch!"

The minute that came out of my mouth, I realized how stupid it sounded. Too late. Ranger Rick and Bert started laughing and whooping.

"Martin, are you alright?" Sadie rushed over, her blue curls bobbing in the breeze as she bent down to take a look at me. She smelled like a mixture of bug spray and floral air freshener.

I stood up and brushed the dirt off my knees, cautiously looking around to see if there was any sign of Sasquatch. He was gone.

"Yes, yes I'm fine," I panted. *Nothing got hurt but my dignity.*

"Sasquatch? Here at Point Beach?" Bert slapped his knee. "That's a real dandy."

"Thanks for the laugh, kid," Ranger Rick sputtered.

Sailor rounded a bend in the trail and raced toward me, arms wide open. She gave me a hug. "I'm so glad you're alright."

We walked off to the side. "What happened? Where's Forest?"

"I don't know." She lowered her voice. "A creepy-looking guy showed up and I tried to warn Forest, but I got scared and took off. I don't know if he made it out in time."

"He won't get caught," I reassured her.

Without warning, someone tapped on my back, and I jumped.

"Hey, remember me?"

I turned around. "Forest!"

"Oh, I see. You ask a guy to risk his life for a harebrained scheme and suddenly you forget all about him?"

Sailor squealed with delight as she squeezed her arms around Forest.

"You made it!" I high fived him. "Did you find anything in the van?"

"Yeah, I found the museum stuff just as you suspected. Odd thing is—they're keeping it all in an old, beat-up suitcase along with a couple of bricks."

Sailor and I huddled in, anxious for the details.

"I didn't want to risk getting caught when I heard Sailor hooting hysterically, so I left everything in the van and hid behind a tree to watch for a while. That's when the other thug showed up. Coyote, I'm guessing."

Forest paused to catch his breath. "When Sasquatch came back, Coyote told him they had to leave soon to meet Badger."

"So there *is* a third accomplice," I deducted.

"Hey, what about your camera, Dominic? Did you get a picture of Sasquatch?" Forest asked.

The camera! I forgot all about it. I dug it out of my pocket, turned it on, and paged back to the image. "Yeah, I got it."

"How'd it turn out?" Sailor leaned in to peek at the picture.

"Awful—" I passed the camera to them. "It looks just like him."

"Hey, this might be the first clear picture of Sasquatch ever taken. We could be famous!" Forest joked.

The laughter from the camp host site finally quieted down as Ranger Rick approached us. "What are you kids up to?"

"We're trying to catch the thieves we heard about in the paper."

Are you kidding me, Sailor? Forest and I gaped at her.

"Oops …" she recanted.

Bert burst anew with laughter. "Girlie, you sure have a good imagination."

Sadie put her hand over her mouth, eyes wide. "Honey, are you saying the Two Rivers thieves are here at Point Beach?"

"You kids tell me right now exactly what you're up to here."

I've seen Ranger Rick annoyed, irritated, and even ruffled, but this marked the first time I saw actual steam blowing out of his ears. What else could we do but tell him?

I began with the raspy voice and the gold tooth. Then Sailor recounted how we picked up Sasquatch and Coyote's frequencies on the walkie-talkies. Finally, Forest told them how we discovered their hiding spot—right here at Point Beach on site #42.

"I don't remember anyone checking in on that site." Ranger Rick wagged a finger.

"It's true," Forest insisted. "Everything they stole from the Washington House is in a suitcase hidden inside their van."

"Yeah, but they'll be gone soon." I raised my hands. "You have to do something!"

Ranger Rick scowled. "Sounds like a bunch of baloney, and this law officer won't be fooled so easily. You three are coming with me." He marched us to his truck.

"Wait—we can prove it to you," Sailor pleaded as she and Forest hesitantly climbed into the back seat. "We have a picture on this camera."

"I have a better idea." Ranger Rick grabbed the camera out of Sailor's hands, shoving me toward the open door. "I'm going to teach you kids what happens when you meddle in other people's business."

I had no choice but to climb in next to them. He slammed the door shut.

CHAPTER 12

The three of us slumped down in the backseat of the DNR truck. This made sense of how agitated the ranger was when he found me with the blue bag on the beach, and how sneaky he acted all the time.

"Buckle up," Ranger Rick ordered. He locked the doors and made a sharp turn out of the driveway, knocking over a few fake palm trees.

No one said a word, though I wondered why he wanted us to put on our seat belts if he meant to "dispose" of us like the rest of the evidence. I shut my eyes, prepared to meet my doom.

The truck skidded to a stop only a minute later.

"So, you're not going to get rid of us?" I looked out the window to find we were still at the campground.

The frown on the ranger's face indicated he was still giving the thought serious consideration.

We were right in front of site #42—but it was completely empty.

"I don't know why I bother with you kids." He scowled.

"They were just here! You have to believe us!" Sailor begged.

"Trying to pull a fast one on a law officer is a serious offense. Don't think you fooled me when I caught you with that bag."

Ranger Rick looked in the rear-view mirror and sighed at the sight of GB and Windsong running up to the truck, waving to get his attention.

"Now what?" Ranger Rick grumbled as he lowered his window.

"Glad we found you, Officer," GB stopped short, baffled at the sight of us inside the truck.

"I'm glad you found me, too. These kids—"

"Now you listen to me, Officer Rick." GB interrupted. He gripped the frame of the truck and leaned in. "We came within inches of being squashed into pancakes by a rusty brown van just a minute ago. I've never seen such reckless driving."

Ranger Rick glanced back at us, then refocused on GB.

"It was a Ford E150 with New York plates on it."

"That's them!" I stared at Ranger Rick as he closed the window and drove away. "You need to stop that van."

My pulse raced. *What if it was too late?*

"Settle down, boy. I'll give the orders around here." He radioed the sheriff's department. "DNR 247—Dispatch."

"Go ahead, 247."

"Requesting backup at the DNR office to detain two suspects from the Washington House robbery. Suspect vehicle is a brown Ford E150 van with New York plates."

"Ten-four, 247."

I'm sure Ranger Rick enjoyed his official duties and played it to the hilt, but to my disappointment he stopped by the camp host site to drop us off, first.

"You kids stay away from the criminals now, and

let the police handle this," the ranger ordered before speeding off.

Sadie stared at us, wide-eyed, while Bert picked up the fallen palm trees.

"Wow, is this really happening?" Sailor squealed with delight. "Can we watch? I mean, from a distance?"

"You heard the ranger. He told you kids to steer clear." Sadie motioned for us to take a seat at the picnic table. "This is a job for the professionals, not children."

Bert ripped open a bag of beef jerky, offering some to us while he struggled to chew on a piece with his loose dentures.

"No, thanks." I glanced at my watch. Time was wasting and I sure wasn't in the mood for beef jerky. About the only reaction he got came from Sprinkles, who stood on her hind legs and started barking.

"Now what?" Forest muttered. "Knowing Ranger Rick, he'll still be trying to plan a stake-out while the crooks slip right past him."

"They're probably long gone by now, anyways." I kicked a rock with my foot which landed on a stack of old newspapers. The top page displayed the headline that spawned the whole investigation:

ICE CREAM BANDITS GET AWAY

That's an understatement.

"Wait a minute." I grabbed the paper to get a closer look. There it was, clear as day—the answer to solving the mystery was under our noses the whole time. "We have to alert Ranger Rick! I know where the crooks are headed!"

"But, Mike …" Sadie started to object.

"And you're a witness. You saw one of them—remember that strange man with the gold tooth?" I said.

"You're right!" Just like that, Sadie scooped up Sprinkles, yelling to Bert, "Start the golf cart. We need to get to the ranger's office, and step on it!"

Bert jumped in and revved the engine. Sadie climbed in next to him, with Sprinkles curled up in a ball on her lap. I grabbed the newspaper and the three of us quickly hopped in the back just in time to notice our grandparents approaching.

"Where are you off to now?" Windsong gaped at

the sight of the five of us and a poodle crammed into a golf cart, but there was no stopping us.

"The office ..." I shouted from the rear-facing backseat. "We'll explain later."

I had to give Mr. Buckley some credit, he didn't dilly-dally around. He took off at breakneck speed, which, in a golf cart, is 15 miles-per-hour. As we rounded the bend, a most welcomed sight greeted us— three patrol cars with flashing red and blue lights. They had the exit blocked, but I didn't see a rusty brown van anywhere.

I jumped out, running toward the police entourage. After I explained everything and showed them the newspaper, one of the officers said, "Good work, kid. We'll inform you as soon as we have the suspects detained."

Two squad cars sped off, sirens blaring, with Ranger Rick's truck trailing behind. One officer remained back at the campground to get a statement. "Alright, we're going to have to take it from the top." He turned to me.

"Sure, but you'll need to talk to all of us, sir. We all helped solve the mystery."

"Yes, indeed. I saw his tooth!" Sadie eagerly reported everything she knew.

"But, Dominic, how did you figure out where the crooks were going?" Sailor interrupted.

"As soon as I noticed this—" I pointed to an article featured right next to the story about the robbery. "The third accomplice wasn't a person named Badger, but the Manitowoc car ferry, *S.S. Badger*."

"Ohhh," she gasped.

"It says here that the *S.S. Badger* was delayed because an engine broke down after it beached on a sand bar. Coyote and Sasquatch had to change their plans and ended up at Point Beach to lie low for a while until it was fixed."

"My guess is they wanted to sink the artifacts to the bottom of the lake to make good on their threat." Forest helped put the pieces together. "Remember I told you about the bricks in the briefcase?"

"Yes—to prove the Two Rivers sundae claim

'won't float,' literally." I affirmed. "Just like the statement they made to the press."

"I hope the bad guys are stopped before it gets thrown overboard." Sailor clasped her hands together.

A call came over the police radio. Sprinkles barked excitedly as Bert started to get out of the cart.

"Folks, I'd appreciate it if you'd just hold tight for now." The officer walked back to the patrol car, then turned to give us a thumbs-up. "They got 'em."

"Oh, happy day, justice has prevailed!" Sadie gave Sprinkles a kiss on her mop head.

"Crime sure doesn't pay," Sailor joined in.

"Well, it does if we collect the reward money," Forest said.

By now, GB and Windsong had pulled up in GB's truck. After seeing us by the flashing light show, their curious expressions quickly changed to concerned.

"Grandpa, we helped catch the Two Rivers robbers—they were camping right here at Point Beach!"

"*What?* Dominic Dorsey! Do you have any idea what kind of danger you put yourself in?"

Windsong clutched Grandpa Bob's arm. They looked to the Buckleys, waiting for an explanation.

"Don't worry. They've been caught, and no one got hurt." Sadie smiled brightly, while Bert leaned back in his seat with a look of satisfaction. But they didn't know GB—I'd be hearing about this for a long time to come.

When the party ended, the police officer escorted Windsong, Forest, and Sailor back to Hipsyville. The Buckleys waved goodbye, and Sprinkles gave one last bark before GB drove me to our campsite.

"I'm starving. All that mystery-solving sure worked up my appetite." I rubbed my empty stomach.

"I'll bet." GB chuckled. We climbed inside Nimrod for some much deserved rest and relaxation.

Tomorrow would be a day to celebrate, and finally put an end to the "Sundae Wars."

CHAPTER 13

Sasquatch and Coyote made headline news, pictured in handcuffs with a policeman reading them their rights.

ICE CREAM ROBBERS GET
THEIR JUST DESSERT

Two brothers from Ithaca, New York, Hank and Harvey Zunker, were taken into custody three days after breaking into the Washington House Museum.

The men attempted to board the S.S. Badger car ferry in Manitowoc, but were apprehended due to a tip from three youths who were camping at the Point Beach State Forest, preventing them from sinking some of Two Rivers' most valuable artifacts. The mayor of Ithaca, whom they claimed hired them, was unavailable for comment.

After the big showdown at Point Beach, it was all anyone could talk about at the 130th Commemoration Ceremony. We rescued the ledger just in time for it to be displayed in Two Rivers' Central Park for the entire world to see.

A newswoman approached GB. "You must be so proud of Dominic and his friends. I understand they figured out that the robbers were hiding at the campground?"

She held the microphone toward him.

"I'm just relieved the good Lord protected Dominic, Forest, and Sailor." GB put his arm around me. "They almost got in some pretty hot water."

"Forest and Sailor? Now those are names you don't hear every day." She smiled at the camera. "Thanks to the teamwork of these three brave, young detectives, the town of Two Rivers can truly celebrate today."

For once, Forest was tongue-tied.

Even Sailor became shy as she gazed bashfully into the camera.

"Oh, I see I'm just in time." Ranger Rick barged in front of us.

The reporter stared at his name tag, then raised her microphone to introduce him. "Officer Rick, I presume? You were in charge of Point Beach during these events, is that correct?"

"Why, yes Ma'am," he gloated. "I keep a pretty tight watch on my campground. Nothing gets past me."

"So much for our TV time," Forest complained. We stepped aside to let Ranger Rick have his moment of glory. "At least we get to collect the reward."

"I know what I'm using my share for. I want you to have it, Grandpa Bob."

GB raised his eyebrows. "What for?"

"To buy a new camper so we can be like everyone else and travel in style."

"That's mighty thoughtful of you, Dominic, but I enjoy using the Nimrod."

Windsong put her arm around me. "You know, Dominic, sometimes being different makes the world a little more interesting."

"Besides," GB's eyes leveled with mine, "I just like spending time with you. Camping in something newer won't change that."

"Okay, Grandpa. Then how about you promise never to make me eat any more SPAM, instead?"

GB chuckled. "Alright. It's a deal."

"I don't really care about the money, either," Sailor chimed in. "Though a little ice cream once in a while would be nice."

"Maybe they could use the reward money to help fix the Washington House."

Was that really Forest talking? I couldn't believe my ears. So, it was unanimous. The reward money would go back to the town.

Just then, the nice lady who GB and I met at the museum made an announcement: "Free sundaes for everyone!" She saw us heading over, and added, "Our heroes are first in line."

Before we could get there, Ranger Rick pushed through the crowd to the front. The ice cream lady winked, then motioned for us to squeeze in behind him.

We gathered together one last time under the camp shelter for 9:00 devotions on Sunday morning before heading back home. A moment of gratitude filled me as I glanced around at the familiar faces: traditional GB, free spirit Windsong, happy-go-lucky Sailor, and tough-nut Forest.

I might even miss that elderly, eccentric couple, Mr. and Mrs. Buckley, and believe it or not, Ranger Rick, too. Our campsite was all cleaned up, and we were ready to go.

"Bye, guys," Windsong called as they started on their way. She blew a kiss to GB. "Hope to hear from you soon, Bobby."

Blushing, GB climbed into the truck.

"Hope to see you next year, Dominic," Sailor hollered as she and Forest waved goodbye.

"You can count on it!" I waved back, watching as they wound down the road in their hipsy caravan. "Have an Illi-nice drive!"

"Come on, Dominic." GB had already started up his polka tunes. "Let's get this show on the road."

It was time to leave, but I couldn't wait to come back to Point Beach again next year.

Debby lives in Maribel, Wisconsin. Along with her children and grandchildren, she is also Mum to her family in Uganda, her mission field. She's a member of Pens of Praise Christian writers' group.

Kate lives in Branch, Wisconsin. She enjoys spending time with her family. She's a church accompanist and member of Pens of Praise Christian writers' group.

Connect with us online at:

www.MysteryatPointBeach.com
Facebook.com/MysteryatPointBeach

Henry Kiryowa Luja is the founder of Bulamu Art Community of Talented Youth, an initiative that offers a platform of expression for young artists. He was raised at Bulamu Children's Village in Uganda, a Christian organization that inspired him to start an apprenticeship program in his community.

You can visit him at: www.Bulamu-Art.com

Our many thanks to family and friends who helped us put this book together. We would especially like to thank Pens of Praise for their ongoing love and support, Ben Wolf, our editor, and Michael Oswald.

Books in the Mystery at Point Beach Series:

Book 1: Sundae Wars
Book 2: Pirate's Booty
Book 3: Alien Invasion
Book 4: Bushwhacked
Book 5: The Ringmaster

Made in the USA
Middletown, DE
18 October 2022

12917262R00071